Featuring Jim Henson's Sesame Street Muppets

A SESAME STREET / GOLDEN PRESS BOOK

Published by Western Publishing Company, Inc. in conjunction with Children's Television Workshop.
© 1985 Children's Television Workshop. Muppet characters © 1985 Muppets, Inc. All rights reserved. Printed in the U.S.A. by
Western Publishing Company, Inc. No part of this book may be reproduced or copied in any form without written permission
from the publisher. Sesame Street®, the Sesame Street sign, and A GROWING-UP BOOK are trademarks and service marks
of Children's Television Workshop. GOLDEN®, GOLDEN & DESIGN®, GOLDEN PRESS®, and A GOLDEN BOOK® are
trademarks of Western Publishing Company, Inc. Library of Congress Catalog Card Number: 84-81594 ISBN 0-307-12014-7/
ISBN 0-307-62114-6 (lib. bdg.)

D E F G H I J

Bert and The Broken Teapot

By Tish Sommers • Illustrated by Diane Dawson Hearn

CTW
SESAME STREET
A GROWING-UP BOOK™

Bert woke up early. He was too excited to go back to sleep.

"Today I'm going to work at Hooper's Store," he told his pet pigeon Bernice. "David has to go to the library, so he said I could help out." Bert whispered so he wouldn't wake up Ernie.

When Bert arrived at the store, David said, "Good
morning! You're right on time. Here's an apron for you
to wear."

Bert slipped the apron on over his head. It fit
perfectly. "Neato," he said.

David showed Bert around the store. He showed him
the refrigerator and the soda fountain and the cookie
jar. Then he took Bert behind the counter and showed
him the teapot on the shelf.

"Please be careful with the teapot," said David. "It is
very special because Mr. Hooper gave it to me."

"Don't worry, David," said Bert. "I'll be as careful with
your teapot as I am with my paper clip collection."

"I'll be back in two hours," David said as he left.
"Take good care of the store!"

"Don't worry about a thing," Bert answered. He set
places at the counter while he waited for his first
customers.

Soon the door opened, and the first customer came in.
"Hi, Bert," Ernie said. "How's it going?"
Bert smoothed his apron. "Fine, Ernie," he said.

The door opened again, and three more customers
came in.

"Hi, Bert. May I have a glass of milk?" Prairie Dawn
asked.

"I'd like some Brussels sprouts," said Herry.

"Cookie, please," said Cookie Monster.

"Coming right up!" said Bert. He knew that was what
David said when he was waiting on customers.

Maria opened the door. "Hi, Bert," she said. She was surprised to see him. "Where's David?"

"He's at the library," Bert told her. "And I'm minding the store."

"David always makes me a cup of tea," said Maria. "Could you do that?"

"You bet, Maria!" said Bert.

"Oh, Bert," said Prairie Dawn. "May I have some more milk, please?"

"Coming right up!" said Bert. Bert was trying to serve his customers as fast as David did. He reached for the milk.

"Watch out for the teapot!" cried Maria.
 But it was too late. Bert knocked the teapot off the
counter. *Crash!* It fell to the floor.

"Oh, no!" cried Bert. "I have broken David's teapot!"
Everyone stared at the pieces on the floor.

"Maybe Luis could fix it," said Prairie Dawn.

"Yeah," said Herry. "I break lots of things, and Luis always fixes them."

"Go ahead, Bert," said Maria. "I'll watch the store while you go to the Fix-it Shop."

Ernie and Bert carefully picked up the pieces and put them in a paper bag.

Bert hurried to the Fix-it Shop. When he got there, Luis was fixing a radio.

"Hi, Bert!" Luis said. "What can I do for you?"

"I was working at Hooper's Store, and I broke David's teapot," Bert told him. He handed Luis the bag full of broken pieces. "Can you fix it for me?"

Luis put the broken pieces on the counter and looked at them.

"I'm sorry, Bert," he said. "The pieces are too small to glue together."

"Are you sure?" Bert asked. Luis nodded his head. "Well...thanks anyway, Luis," Bert said. He left the Fix-it Shop. He felt very sad.

Bert wandered down Sesame Street, wondering what to do.

"Hey, you with the pointy head!" Oscar called as Bert passed the trash can. "You look sad and miserable–really great! What happened?"

Bert held out the paper bag full of broken pieces. "This was David's special teapot," he said, "and I broke it."

Oscar peered into the bag. "It's beautiful!" he said. "Want to trade?"

Oscar disappeared into his trash can and slammed the lid shut. A minute later he popped up, holding his favorite grouch teapot. It was cracked and broken.

"It's great for making hot mud with marshmallows," Oscar said.

Bert sighed. "Thanks anyway, Oscar," he said. "I don't think it would take the place of the teapot Mr. Hooper gave David."

"What will I tell David?" Bert wondered as he walked past 123 Sesame Street.

"Hi, Bert," Big Bird called from his nest. "Why are you so sad?"

"I was minding the store for David, and I broke his special teapot," Bert told him.

"Oh." Big Bird thought for a minute. "Hey!" he said. "I have something that keeps water hot. Maybe you could give it to David in place of his teapot."

Big Bird reached into his nest and pulled out a bright red hot-water bottle.

Bert shook his head sadly. "I don't think so, Big Bird," he said. "But thanks anyway."

Bert walked slowly back to Hooper's Store. He slipped off the apron, folded it, and sat down to wait for David. "Now David will never let me work in the store again," he thought. "And maybe he won't be my friend any more, either."

"Hi, Bert! I'm back!" David said. "How's it going?"

Bert took a deep breath. "I broke your teapot, David. I was trying to serve the customers as fast as you do, and I knocked it off the counter." He showed David the broken pieces.

"I'm sorry," said Bert, trying not to cry.

David sat down on the stool next to Bert. "I think I know how you feel," said David. "I used to help Mr. Hooper in the store when I was a little boy. One day I broke his favorite cookie jar. And do you know what he said to me?"

"What?" asked Bert.

"Mr. Hooper said, 'My friend David is more important to me than any cookie jar.'" David smiled. "And you know what, Bert?"

"What?" asked Bert.

"My friend Bert is more important to me than any teapot," said David.

"I'll buy you a new teapot," Bert said bravely. "I'll save
my money, and maybe I can sell my paper clip collection."
"I have a better idea," said David.
"What's that?" asked Bert.

"You can help me in the store again next Saturday," David said.

"Do you mean it, David?" asked Bert. "Groovy! I will try not to break anything ever again. I promise I will be very careful."

"I know you will," said David.